To

JAMES

FROM

Anaelle

Written by JD Green
Illustrated by Jennifer Naalchigar
Designed by Nicola Moore

First published by HOMETOWN WORLD in 2018
Hometown World Ltd
7 Northumberland Buildings
Bath
BA1 2JB

www.hometownworld.co.uk

Follow us @hometownworldbooks

ISBN 978-1-78553-797-4

Printed in Malta
HTW_PO010917

JAMES YOU'RE AMAZING!

Hometown World

James is so **AMAZING**.

The nicest, smartest guy.

He's **super cool** (and cool kids rule).

It's true! I'll tell you why...

James is very **helpful**.

He gives this mix a beating.

And when that cake's had time to bake,

he'll help out **with**

the

eating.

James is very **caring**.

He's friend to birds and bees,

and **bugs**, and **slugs**, and dogs, and frogs,

and even **cats with fleas!**

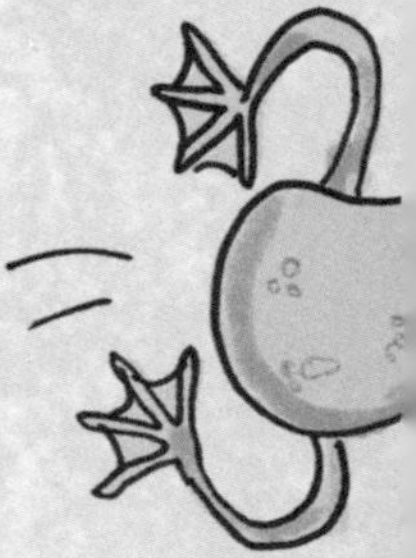

James is quite a **rock star!**

Each time he hears a song,

he sings aloud but does not care

if all the words are wrong!

James has such a lovely smile

that goes from ear to ear.

Just spending time around him

leaves you feeling full of cheer.

James is such a **smart** boy.
Of that I have no doubt!
He pulls the plug and studies how
the bathwater drains out!

James is very **sporting**.

You'll always see him **grinning**.

He won't cry if he **loses**
and he won't boast if he's **winning!**

Not **everything** comes easily.
He practises **a lot!**
And that's how he's developed
the **AMAZING** skills he's got.

PHEW!

HEY STANLEY!

James is such a
brave boy.

This spider's
not a threat!

He picks it up,
gives it a name

and keeps it as
his pet!

There's always **fun** and **laughter**

everywhere James goes.

He likes to dance around a lot

and strike a funky pose...

SO FUN!

James is very **generous**

with all his awesome toys.

He shares them out when playing with

the other **girls** and **boys**.

THE BEST!

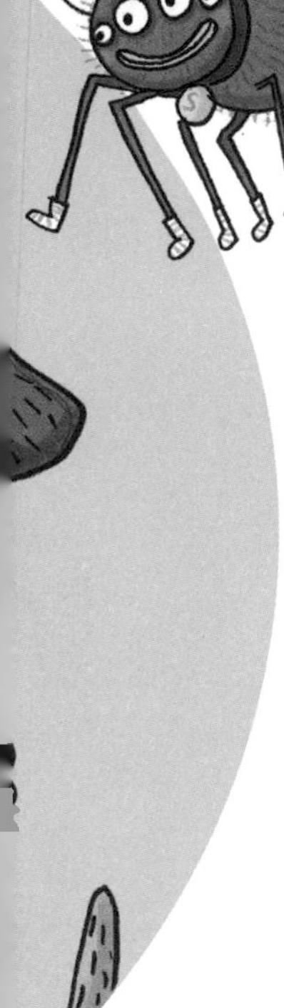

James is so **AMAZING**.

What sets this boy apart

is that he's **cool**, and **brave**, and **fun**,

and has a ***GREAT***

BIG

HEART!

Add some more AMAZING words about YOU!